VENI VIDI VICI

A SECURITY DIRECTORATE SHORT STORY

ALEXANDRIA BLAELOCK

Also by Alexandria Blaelock

SHORT STORY COLLECTIONS
The Histories of Hayward Hall
Lovelorn, Lovestruck and Love at First Sight
Common or Garden Variety Heroes
Case Files of the Wilkinson Detective Agency
Unavoidable Fates
Christmas Travesties
Five Faces of Felicia Clarke
Little Place Called Home

FICTION
That Love Nonsense
Taipan vs Brown
The Ghost and Ms Cox
Friends Like That

MS BLAELOCK'S BOOKS
Stress Free Dinner Parties
Signature Wardrobe Planning
Holistic Personal Finance
Minimally Viable Housekeeping
Planning a Life Worth Living

A SELECTION OF AVAILABLE SHORT STORIES
Alma's Grace
Fate in Your Hands
Lady of the Looking Glass
Morning Star, Evening Star, Superstar
Secret Singer
Shining Star
Ship in a Bottle
Simone Says Hands in the Air
The Day the Schedule Broke

VENI VIDI VICI

A SECURITY DIRECTORATE SHORT STORY

ALEXANDRIA BLAELOCK

BlueMere Books
MELBOURNE, AUSTRALIA

For permission requests, please contact enquiries@bluemerebooks.com.

Ordering Information:
Discounts are available on quantity purchases. For details, contact orders@bluemerebooks.com.

Veni Vidi Vici/Alexandria Blaelock
paperback ISBN: 978-1-922744-86-9
digital ISBN: 978-1-922744-87-6

Book Layout © BookDesignTemplates.com
Cover Art © grandfailure/Depositphotos

VENI VIDI VICI

Cora was a Eugenics Programme success. She'd passed the Genomics Bureau post-natal testing, survived the State Academy of Cultural Regulation with a useful genetic "superpower" and graduated from the University of Civilisation with an advantageous qualification.

So spending the next few weeks manually weeding the vegetable bed, pruning the fruit trees, and keeping the lush growth of whatever the prickly native vegetation was under control was bad enough without alarms going off to boot.

She'd more or less just arrived at Exploratorem Station, and despite all the drills, hadn't heard that particular sequence of tones, and didn't know what it meant.

Alert or alarmed?

Evacuate quickly or assemble nearby and return slowly?

Grab a gun and prepare for invasion?

It was vexing.

Had she just gone through the most useless induction on the planet?

Security clearances notwithstanding, surely the most basic of site education programmes should include identification and explanation of all alarm codes.

She frowned and inspected her chafed and blister scarred hands as she stood, stretching out her aching back and arms while looking around to see what the others were doing.

There was not a human to be seen, only the open fields of red dirt bisected by waist height fences made of dried offcuts of the cut back native vegetation. Towards the distance, a small, faded green corrugated tin tool shed with a gable roof at the entrance to the productive gardens, and further off in the distance, the station itself.

Criminal to leave her out here on her own.

The point of newbies and returnees working in the fields was not just food production. It was acclimatising as quickly as possible to the altitude, the climate, and the air-borne spores that were toxic to some.

Which meant someone should be here supervising her.

If she could not adjust, the local command needed to isolate and treat her before sending her back to the City on the next convoy out for redeployment.

Assuming she was fit to take up another post and avoid an untimely transfer to the Euthanasia Programme.

This lack of supervision was negligent.

Then again, she was a recent graduate - a very new, very junior officer, so perhaps this was just code for some stupid hazing ritual. Leave her alone and set off some kind of alarm.

Watch, laughing, from the control room to see what she did.

She frowned for a moment, then looked more attentively around her.

The air was clear; no sign of environmental or surface disturbances.

Birds sang in the fencing and trees, so nothing unusual enough to send them squawking away in alarm.

The light breeze drying her sweaty brow smelled pleasantly floral. No hint of smoke or chemical contaminants.

Except for the scentless, tasteless, invisible spores she was here to interact with, there didn't appear to be any danger.

No reason to return to base, no reason to evacuate, no reason to take action at all.

So, if this was a hazing ritual, there'd probably be some kind of embarrassing prank set up for her when she returned to base. Some sort of physical trial that would set off alarms, spray her with something unpleasant or staining, or just plain running the gauntlet while her new colleagues attempted to land a punch, kick, or noxious projectile.

Maybe some other painful and humiliating scenario that would dog her for the rest of her career.

Irritating.

She curled her lip.

Best keep working until the lunch break, then stun them with her equanimity when she returned to base. If the alarm was something urgent or important, no doubt an officer would send for her.

Annoyed as well as stubborn, she bent once more to her weeding. At this point, she didn't have a security clearance, so diligent work on her assigned task would probably earn more credit than standing around gawping and getting in the way.

Regardless of the state of her hands, back and legs.

Not forgetting her brain, which seemed to be stagnating.

But given the usual environmental conditions weren't the best for growing, you had to get out and work the fields while you could.

Unsocial at the best of times, she'd found Exploratorem's spartan life suited her.

A minimal crew, living a monastic lifestyle. Limited communication with the outside world, though Cora didn't yet know whether that was something to do with the location or some kind of security embargo she hadn't been told about yet.

Everyone on the crew, except maybe the station director, rotated through several standard shifts over the days, weeks and months. Aside from their regular assigned duties, there was hard physical labour in the fields growing the food.

Then time spent cooking and preserving the food and brewing beer, maintenance of equipment and machinery, plus the random security and evacuation drills.

Which made it all the more curious; why didn't she know what this alarm meant.

Was it another security clearance blockage?

While it felt insulting, there wasn't much point learning more about what the station did until they all knew she'd be completing her assignment rather than heading back to the City.

When her posting was announced, a murmur had run through the University auditorium.

Everyone had heard of Exploratorem, and the harsh life endured there, but no one knew precisely what function Exploratorem performed.

Wild rumours about activities like covert surveillance, interrogations and mind control were everywhere, but given you weren't supposed to talk about your work, that was probably just trash talk filling the vacuum of fact.

She couldn't help feeling a little smug that she was the one who was going to find out.

Cora's "superpower" was influence. She couldn't control minds *per se*, but she could encourage them to *lean* in a particular direction. It didn't surprise her that the future would involve her power - it was what she'd trained for, after all.

And having just scraped past her physical final, Cora knew she wasn't going to the station for anything other than her brilliant mind.

Most people took one look at her petite busty body, and that was that. She owned them, no need to consider the application of her superpower.

Her unusually bright green eyes snared those who looked higher, some even noticing their setting in a cute, heart-shaped face surrounded by long, wavy blonde hair.

However, those who assumed she was a pushover were generally surprised to find otherwise, but not for long.

Her outer beauty disguised an icy heart, ruthless spirit and steel spine. She was a triumph of social conditioning.

She'd worked hard to build up her dumb blonde persona with revealing clothes and a breathy voice. It allowed her to more easily manipulate her opponents and gave her the element of surprise when leveraged with her quick reflexes.

Though the amount of physical labour she'd endured in the fields and kitchens during the last couple of weeks had not only improved the quality of her sleep, but her muscle strength and tone too.

Plus, she'd gained a light tan that made her look as healthy as she felt, though she could've done without the freckles that now sprinkled her nose.

But they added to her armoury; in the right circumstances, they'd be disarming.

Shame she hadn't been this fit for the physical final, though if she'd done better, who knew where she'd be now?

And she had the feeling that Exploratorem was going to be right up her alley.

Cora lugged her trug of weeds to the compost heap and emptied it.

Was life at the station austere to keep the mind sharp, or was it an intensive boot camp style muscle building training camp preparing junior officers for some other placement?

Given her power, an assassin perhaps?

The siren for lunch finally sounded.

Cora collected her tools together, cleaned and stowed them in the tool shed before dusting her hands off on the legs of her boiler suit and walking towards the station.

As she got closer, she felt her heart rate increase in anticipation of the hazing prank and started looking more carefully for triggers. But it all seemed perfectly normal until she reached the squat, concrete sentry box.

The marine inside did not challenge her as he had done every other time she'd returned from the fields. In fact, he didn't acknowledge her in any way. Just sat at silent attention, staring out the window, not meeting her gaze.

Not moving a muscle.

She rapped on the window, but he didn't flinch or even look at her.

Her annoyance was increasing; given everything else, she was at threat level three at this point.

He was just a goon, after all. At the very least, he should acknowledge her as his superior with a nod or a "ma'am".

She could understand why the more senior officers might choose to haze her, but goons as well? This was beyond a joke.

She stalked around the box and ripped the door open.

He fell backwards out of the box, tumbling off his seat onto the ground.

Cora jumped back on guard, expecting him to rise and attempt to subdue her, but he lay where he fell.

She stretched her leg out and poked him with a safety booted toe, but he remained unresponsive.

Somewhat reassured, she crouched and checked his pulse.

It took her several attempts to realise he didn't have a pulse.

Curious.

But annoyingly extreme for a prank.

When she took the news back to the station, what would they want to know?

Cora examined the body. Its uniform and boots were clean, crisp, and intact. There were no visible signs of trauma, smelling of standard-issue soap. There didn't seem to be anything to indicate a cause of death.

She moved onto the sentry box. No visible damage internally or externally. No sign of a spill, electrical malfunction, or tampering. Aside from her boot prints, there was no disturbance to the ground.

All in all, nothing to suggest causality.

She reached into the box and picked up the radio handset, clicking the call button a couple of times to attract attention from the station.

There was no response.

She didn't yet know Exploratorem's security protocols, but more widely, radio communications required the receiver to acknowledge transmission and engage scrambling before communication could commence.

She clicked the call button another couple of times.

Still no response.

She ground her teeth.

Idiots, all of them.

Was this still a prank, or, given the dead soldier something more serious?

She put the radio handset back in its place and, leaving the body where it was, headed into the prickly native vegetation alongside the road for a more circumspect approach to the main station building.

As she prowled through the bush, she was alert to changes in the environment, but the conditions remained as innocuous as when the alarm first sounded.

Aside from the dead marine and unresponsive radio, there was nothing to suggest that this day was any different from any other she'd spent here.

Perhaps something like this scenario had been the basis of her final physical exam. She'd learnt a lot from her debriefing, but hadn't expected to be an unarmed one-woman assault party on her own station.

At least not anytime soon anyway.

With only a few metres to go, she slowed her pace still further and examined the station façade.

The walls were smooth and unbroken, the gravel of the road and car park were no more choppy than usual. Three station all-terrain vehicles parked in an orderly row down one side of the parking area. Doors were all neatly closed with no evidence of attack, abrupt arrival or departure.

All as expected, with no signs of an external assault.

That didn't rule out a quick, clean, surgical assault with enemy agents waiting inside the station, but it made that scenario less likely.

From her limited political knowledge, the only viable enemy was rebels, and they were scum who didn't have the organisation, aptitude or technical skills for a precision strike.

Which, assuming the goon did not die of natural causes, left either an armed internal assault or some kind of silent chemical or electrical attack.

Was there such a thing that could simultaneously disable both the station and a moron in a box a few hundred metres away?

An electromagnetic pulse could disable the equipment, but was there something similar that could disable people too?

Human brains were mostly electric, so theoretically, it was possible to do both. She hadn't heard of this kind of weapon as an actual device, or in development, but you'd need a security clearance of the highest level to know for sure.

If such a device had been deployed at Exploratorem, would it have fired once or still be "on?"

Though if it were on, she wouldn't have made it this far, so she probably didn't need to worry about her brain frying from the inside out.

In any case, she couldn't stand around out there all day. She had to get inside the station before she could determine her next steps.

It was possible she'd avoided detection to this point, but thanks to not having a security clearance, she'd no choice but to enter via the front door. If whoever it was didn't know she was here now, they soon would.

And if they knew she was there, they'd be expecting her to arrive for lunch anyway.

Hopefully, this was the most meticulously planned and implemented hazing prank ever known in the Security Directorate.

But just in case, she set her hair loose and fluffed it up before pulling the zipper of her boiler suit down a little lower to expose the lace edges of her bra. Deciding that wasn't enough, she rolled her sleeves and pants up to reveal a little more skin.

She pulled a small branch of leaves from a nearby tree, then popped back onto the road and starting walking leisurely towards the station, swinging her hips and fanning herself with the branch.

Looking like a sexy, and clueless woman on a day trip to the country.

Her influence was the most effective at close quarters, and completely ineffective when viewed on a screen at a distance. Even so, she generated an influence of "poor, lazy little rich girl, completely out of her depth."

It might not help with those in the station, but it reminded her she had a persona to work with.

Her skinned crawled, and her heart was beating like crazy, but there wasn't really an alternative to walking in the open.

The closer she got to the station, the harder it was to force her body to keep moving forward.

Bit of a shame she couldn't influence herself as easily as others.

Arriving at the front door without challenge, when she held her security card over the reader, it surprised her to find it already open.

It was possible the entry security system was separate from the primary system, but not likely.

So if the security was working, the entire station should be too.

She pushed open the door to find the entryway empty. She took a long step sideways into a corner and stood still and silent to listen.

Aside from the buzz of the single light flickering, all was quiet.

At this time of day, she should've been able to hear the murmur of conversation. There should be computers pinging when they picked up whatever they were looking for. There should be phones and printers and drawers slamming.

But aside from her beating heart, all was quiet.

Cora felt as though her skin had crawled right off her body, leaving all her nerves exposed.

Whatever was going on felt very, very wrong.

And given that, she'd feel a whole lot better with a gun in her hand.

Next stop, the armoury, which fortunately was just around the corner.

She sidled along the corridor, back to the wall, generating an "I'm not here" influence. She didn't see anyone, living or dead, as she inched around the corner towards the armoury.

Risking exposure, she ducked her head through the doorway and saw an armourer slumped over the counter, but nothing else was obviously suspicious.

She stepped into the room, tensed on her toes, ready to leap back. The armourer remained static; no projectiles fired in her direction.

Nothing happened.

Looking as closely as she could at the room, given the flickering light from the hall, she found nothing that seemed unusual.

Or more unusual than this already unusual situation, at any rate.

She took the armourer's pulse, and he too did not have one.

Station policy required guns be sealed in the cage behind the armourer's counter, and she would (of course) not have access. Taking a step back, she vaulted across the desk and slid to the ground behind it, dislodging the armourer in the process.

He fell to the floor with a crash, and she dived for cover under a bar set up for cleaning the guns.

She forced herself to be still, and blood pounding in her ears, she took a deep breath and held it while she slowly counted.

One.

Two.

Three.

Four.

Five.

Six.

Seven.

Eight.

Nine.

Ten.

No alarms, no movement.

She let her breath out in a big sigh, enjoying the momentary feeling of relief as her shoulders dropped and the built-up tension in her body released.

Then she pulled herself to her feet, grabbed a rifle from a rack and rummaged around looking for preloaded magazines. One for the rifle, locked and loaded, plus a bunch in the pockets of her suit.

While she didn't really think this was a prank any longer, if it was, she didn't want her colleagues thinking she wasn't willing to do what had to be done to save them.

And in fact, by this point, she was so annoyed she really hoped there was someone out there to viciously shoot up.

As she opened the door of the armoury cage, she noticed the armourer's body again.

The station was climate controlled, and she had no idea whether the air was canned or mixed with fresh air from outside.

What if it had been a chemical attack or spill and there was some poisonous residue still circulating in the station's air?

Worst-case scenario, something like poison tainted the air, and she would die before she could alert the Director General's Office.

How pathetic.

Best-case scenario, she shouldered a re-breather and saved the day.

She grabbed a re-breather and pulled it on as she walked towards the corridor, psyching herself up to step back into it.

She briefly considered calling out to the station crew for assistance, but the gut instincts that ensured she survived the Academy of Cultural Regulation were telling her not to draw attention to herself.

The next target should probably be the control centre, to see if it was operational and whether there was any data about the incident.

Or, given that there was a limit to what one short junior officer without a security clearance could do, external communication back to the City.

As you'd expect, it was a secure panic room style office in the centre of the building. And she didn't know the exact path to find it.

Or whether she'd be able to gain entry.

Thanks for nothing Security Chief.

But if this was a "situation," and if they needed help, she had to get to the control room.

Radiating her "I'm not here" influence, Cora sidled out of the room and back into the corridor.

At first, the corridors were clear, but as she neared the mess hall, rifle at the ready, she started seeing the bodies of her colleagues. Sprawled haphazardly, as if a puppet master had just cut their strings.

She stopped to examine the first few to find that, like the marine and armourer, they had no pulse and no obvious cause of death.

Losers, all of them.

With no external air getting through the re-breather, Cora couldn't tell whether there was food cooking or burning, so she checked the kitchen to see if there was any sign of what time the incident, whatever it was, had occurred.

Even more bodies were piled up in the mess, but she didn't bother to give them more than a cursory glance to see if any were moving.

Similarly, the kitchen contained several bodies. One had collapsed over the grill was charring gently, so she pulled him off it in case he set the place on fire.

Forgetting she wasn't wearing a watch; she checked her wrist against the kitchen clock and made a note to never take it off again.

She checked a random body to find its watch matched the clock. Going by how hungry she was, she deduced the clock had the right time.

Food was prepped and ready to cook, but cooking hadn't begun. Which suggested the incident had occurred sometime between mid-morning and the first lunch service. Maybe an hour or two ago.

And given people had died on their way into the mess, it probably wasn't something in the food.

Cora turned to leave the kitchen through the other door and noticed a rat by the wall. Giving it a poke with the rifle barrel, she wasn't really surprised that it didn't move. Though the rigidity of its body compared to those of the crew was surprising.

She remembered reading somewhere that rodents go outside to die. So was it possible that contamination in the air system had slowly built to a dose lethal to humans?

Though if that was the case, how had the marine died in the sentry box a few hundred metres away?

A slow-acting poison?

Cora massaged her temples before snuggling the rifle back into her shoulder and heading out.

The still emptiness of the usually noisy, bustling station was unsettling. Not to mention the piles of inexplicably dead people.

She was finding it more difficult to control her emotions and feeling her self-control slipping.

A while later, after walking up and down a few more corridors, she came across the control room door.

At least, the red-lit room full of brightly lit screens and panels of flashing lights seen through the window of the double blast doors looked like it might be a control room.

It could have been a decoy room, but the bodies slumped over the computer terminals suggested the room had a legitimate purpose.

Not that it mattered. She had to get in.

But first, a quick reconnoitre up and back the corridor looking for concealed enemy agents.

Not that there was much in the way of hiding places, aside from more unmarked corpses.

Trying not to shudder, she focused on the access panel next to the door.

It was a large panel with access modes including card reader, PIN keypad, hand reader, and retinal scanner.

And a steadily glowing red light.

There was no way she was going to be able to break the door down, so the only option was to try the access controls one by one and see what happened.

Tucking the rifle under her armpit, and crossing her fingers, she swiped her card. The light flashed green for a moment along with what seemed, in the silence, a deafening beep.

She pulled the door, but nothing happened.

Next, she tried the PIN she used to access her sleeping quarters, and again the light flashed green with a beep.

But still the door didn't open.

"Fuck."

She let out a sigh and looked up at the ceiling.

She rubbed her sweaty right hand down the leg of her pants and placed it on the reader.

It was cool to the touch, but started heating up rapidly.

She knew this was a tool to warn off unauthorised personnel, and also knew that if she wasn't authorised, the pad would continue to heat until she removed her hand or it burned her skin off.

She was just about at the point where the pain was too great to continue when the light flashed and the device beeped.

Cora snatched her hand back and pressed it to her breast until the pain lessened.

She pulled the door, and it still didn't open.

"Fuck's sake!"

She stamped a little dance and kicked the door violently several times.

Then groaned and laid her forehead against the door. There was no choice now but to try the retina scanner.

If they hadn't transferred her retinal print to the station, or hadn't authorised it, the scanner would blind her.

And more or less useless for the current incident and perhaps the rest of her career.

But there was no other way.

She had to try.

Not that they gave you medals for trying.

She took a deep breath, squeezed her eyes shut, and counted to ten.

Then, before she could change her mind, she put her face in front of the scanner and tried not to flinch as the laser flashed for what seemed like eternity and her vision failed her.

She closed her eyes, trying not to sob, trying not to think about a one-dimensional future with an eye patch.

Then she heard a beep and a clunk as the door unlocked.

A single tear escaped her eye and slid down her cheek.

She opened her eyes; and found she could see. Just momentarily dazzled by the brightness of the laser.

But there was no time for hysterics. She had a job to do.

Despite her success at gaining entry to the control room, she was a little embarrassed to find she could probably have gained entrance more or less any time she wanted. It was a testament to the strength of her training that she hadn't tried.

Or had someone inside set it up as they were dying?

Was the alarm that sounded a keep clear alert?

She took a deep breath and pulled the door open.

A cursory glance found still, unmarked bodies slumped where they'd fallen. She didn't notice any countdowns or screen displays that suggested she'd only a few seconds to do something sensational before the station self-destructed.

She relaxed a little. All she had to do now was find the communications desk and get a message out.

Walking through the desks, she pushed and pulled bodies away from the terminals here and there until she found the one she needed. She set her rifle on the desk, pushed the body from its chair and sat down.

As expected, the computer was locked, but she forced a restart.

Drumming her fingers on the desk, willing it to go faster.

She leaned forward and was monetarily stunned by a heavy blow to the back of her neck, smacking her head on the desk.

Rolling off the chair, she looked up to see a figure in an environmental suit going for the rifle.

It wasn't her intention to get this far to be disabled before she could get the message out.

Struggling to make her eyes focus and get her brain to kick back in, she tried to generate an influence that would suggest to the figure that the gun was going to be more of a hindrance than a help.

She was successful in that the jerk turned its attention back to her, but that meant it was trying to kill her where she lay.

A mixed blessing.

Flailing about on the floor, she was trying to regain her footing, press an attack, and continue to generate a useful influence.

As the adrenaline kicked in, so did her training, and she could get to her feet and more effectively parry the undisciplined blows of her opponent.

Time seemed to slow down, and in the gaps between the seconds, Cora influenced the level of panic in her opponent so that it became more confused and less coordinated.

As it lost its ability to mount an effective defence, she influenced further, to reduce its confidence in itself.

It was enough to give her the break she needed to force it backwards, grab the rifle and fire.

It was outraged, and came at her with renewed vigour and a loud roar, so she fired again and again, emptying the magazine into it.

She backed away as it kept coming, pulling out the spent magazine and dropping it on the floor as she pulled a replacement from her pocket.

As she was shoving the new magazine into place, her opponent slipped on the spent one and crashed into the desk, sending computer equipment flying everywhere.

It rolled off the desk and lay still on the floor.

She hoped that 30 bullets were enough to keep it down, but backed further away, trying to work out how she'd stupidly missed someone in an environmental suit during her initial inspection of the room.

A glance around the room revealed that part of the wall was, in fact, a concealed door, still ajar, so she ducked low and skirted the edges of the control room until she got there.

It was the Director's office, and it was a mess.

The desk and chair overturned, papers and computer equipment strewn around the room as if a madman had turned the place over in some kind of fit.

More significantly, the Director was not in it.

Was it the Director who'd attacked her?

And why was he wearing an environmental suit?

Was he the one who'd attacked the station?

But why?

She returned to the control room, half expecting the body in the suit to have disappeared, but it lay where she'd left it.

In an attractively spreading pool of blood.

After hefting it with a solid kick to be sure it was dead, she pulled the suit helmet off to find it was the Director, his eyes wide, with dilated pupils. A smear of blood had dried below his nostrils.

What the fuck?

Was he a rebel or something?

At that point, she almost gave up, but despite everything, she needed to contact the Director General's office.

Apart from all other concerns, she needed to eat, and there was no telling what might be safe.

She sighed and rubbed the back of her neck where the Director had hit her.

Reluctantly putting down her rifle again, she picked up the bits of computer equipment and plugged them back together.

She'd never influenced technology before, but she closed her eyes and placed both hands near the equipment, telling it to work. Then she took a deep breath and pushed the on button.

It whirred compliantly.

While she'd made it this far, Cora still knew nothing more than the most general of basic security protocols, so that was what she'd have to use.

Crossing her fingers, she logged into the Directorate network and pinged the Director General's office, requesting a secure channel.

Hopefully, the Exploratorem initiation code would be sufficient for her to be shunted through to someone who could help.

The adrenalin was wearing off, and the stress of the day was catching up with her. She was suddenly exhausted. She found her head bobbing as she dozed off, woken by a voice from the computer, "Attention Second Lieutenant Meadows."

Her head snapped upright as she surged out of the chair to attention.

"At ease Lieutenant."

She resumed her seat.

"What is the situation Meadows."

Not game to take the re-breather off. Cora pointed at it and quickly typed her response, "everyone dead

"director tried to halt comms

"had to kill."

"One moment please," the officer at the other end said.

Tinny music came through the speaker as the screen dissolved into a swirl of colour, pulsating in time with the music.

Cora leaned back in her chair, stretching.

A burst of static and she was face-to-face with General Bruce. She remained seated, but saluted.

"Well done Meadows.

"My adjutant is organising a relief mission. We're sending choppers in. You'll have help by dinnertime."

She nodded once.

"You'll start hearing some noises as we take control of the environmental and security systems from here, but I assure you, you'll be perfectly safe."

She nodded again.

A cool breeze caressed her face, and she typed "air moving now."

"Good. Your re-breather may be compromised, so please keep it on until you get outside."

Cora nodded once.

"I know it's not your speciality, but do you have any theories about the cause of the deaths? It will help the incoming troops decide where to start."

She started typing again, in full sentences given who she was "talking" to, "the dead include rodents, station personnel and at least one sentry outside. The Director was wearing an environmental suit. Perhaps chemical or EM pulse."

"I'll pass that along."

"Thank you sir."

"In the meantime, wait outside for the relief troops to arrive."

"Thank you sir."

The General looked towards someone sitting on his left, nodded once and turned his attention back to her.

"We have control of the situation now. You are dismissed."

She nodded and saluted. The General returned the salute, and the Security Directorate screen saver appeared on the screen.

Taking the rifle with her, she left the station, removed the re-breather and returned to the fields. She'd snack on some fruit, and take a nap while she waited.

THE END

ABOUT THE AUTHOR

Alexandria Blaelock writes stories, some of them for *Ellery Queen's Mystery Magazine* and *Pulphouse Fiction Magazine*.

She's also written five selfhelp books applying business techniques to personal matters like getting dressed, cleaning house, and feeding your friends.

She lives in a forest because she enjoys birdsong, and the smell of gum leaves. When not telecommuting to parallel universes from her Melbourne based imagination, she watches K-dramas, talks to animals, and drinks Campari. At the same time.
Discover more at www.alexandriablaelock.com.

... or the collections

Why not try The Ghost and Ms Cox

Life interrupted

To say the letter was a surprise was an understatement. It arrived addressed to Miss Finlay Cox, which made the contents even more extraordinary.

Orphan Finn Cox inherits a cottage. Thinks it holds the key to her origins. Of course she takes a look. Who wouldn't?

But when she gets there, she gets more than she bargained for.

Is it friend, family or foe?

www.ingramcontent.com/pod-product-compliance
Lightning Source LLC
Chambersburg PA
CBHW031258210726

48287CB00003B/1082